DISNEP
✦ PRINCESS

CINDERELLA

A Story of Perseverance

W9-CFJ-661

Adapted by Amy Adair
Illustrated by the Disney Storybook Artists

©Disney Enterprises, Inc. All Rights Reserved.

This publication may not be reproduced in whole or in part by any means whatsoever without written permission from the copyright owners. Permission is never granted for commercial purposes.

Published by Louis Weber, C.E.O., Publications International, Ltd.
7373 North Cicero Avenue, Lincolnwood, Illinois 60712

Ground Floor, 59 Gloucester Place, London W1U 8JJ

Customer Service: 1-800-595-8484 or customer_service@pilbooks.com

www.pilbooks.com

p i kids is a registered trademark of Publications International, Ltd.

Manufactured in China.

8 7 6 5 4 3 2 1

ISBN-13: 978-1-4127-6774-3

ISBN-10: 1-4127-6774-1

publications international, ltd.

Once upon a time, there lived a girl named Cinderella. Cinderella's Stepmother and stepsisters, Drizella and Anastasia, were very cruel. Cinderella did all the chores. She even served the Stepmother and stepsisters breakfast in bed. Every morning, she carefully balanced three trays and carried them up the stairs.

Cinderella was miserable being a servant to her Stepmother and stepsisters, but she always did her chores as cheerfully as she could. She knew that someday she would find happiness, even if she had to work doubly hard to find it.

Luckily Cinderella did have some wonderful friends — the sweet little mice and birds who kept her company when she was lonely. The mice and birds also wanted Cinderella to find happiness.

In the castle not far away, the King worried. He wanted to see his son, the Prince, fall in love and marry. "We will host a ball," the King said. "I hope the Prince will find his true love there."

That afternoon, a royal messenger knocked on Cinderella's door. He handed her an envelope. Cinderella gave the envelope to her stepmother.

"Every maiden must attend the royal ball," the Stepmother read.

"That means I can go," Cinderella said.

"You can go if you finish your chores," the Stepmother said slyly. "And if you can find something suitable to wear."

Cinderella worked and worked to finish all her chores, but her cruel Stepmother just gave Cinderella more to do!

Exhausted, Cinderella went to her room and opened the trunk she had been given long ago. She found her old pink dress. If she worked quickly, she was sure she could mend it. But before she could sew a single stitch, her horrible stepsisters cried, "Cinderella! Get here this instant!"

Jaq and Gus, two mice, knew Cinderella would never be able to finish her dress in time. Together with the other mice and the birds, they snipped and stitched and did it for her.

When it was finished, they showed the dress to Cinderella. It was beautiful! But when Cinderella's stepsisters saw the dress, they were filled with jealousy. They tore the pretty dress and ruined it. Cinderella would not be able to go to the ball.

Cinderella ran to the garden and cried. Then Cinderella's Fairy Godmother appeared!

"Dry your eyes," the Fairy Godmother said. "What you need is a pumpkin."

Suddenly, a small pumpkin appeared and grew into a beautiful carriage. Then the Fairy Godmother turned Jaq and Gus into horses.

The Fairy Godmother waved her wand, and Cinderella was wearing an elegant ball gown. She was also wearing delicate glass slippers.

"On the final stroke of midnight, the spell will be broken," the Fairy Godmother warned Cinderella. "Everything will be as it was before."

"Thank you, Fairy Godmother," Cinderella called gratefully as she climbed into the carriage.

When Cinderella entered the ballroom, everyone turned to stare at her, including the Prince. She was the most beautiful maiden there. The Prince refused to dance with anyone else, and everyone watched as the two gracefully twirled to the music.

"Who is she?" someone asked.

"I've never seen her before," said another.

The Stepmother peered through the crowd at the mysterious girl dancing with the dashing Prince. "There is something very familiar about her," she said.

Cinderella forgot about the Fairy Godmother's warning until she heard the clock chime the first stroke of midnight.

"I must go!" she said, turning to run.

The Prince tried to follow Cinderella, but all the other maidens in the ballroom stopped him.

Cinderella ran down the castle steps, accidentally leaving one of her glass slippers behind. Her carriage hurried away, and on the final stroke of midnight, the spell was broken. But Cinderella still had the other glass slipper.

The next day, the King ordered every maiden in the kingdom to try on the left-behind glass slipper. The Prince hoped to find his true love this way.

In the meantime, the Stepmother figured out that it was Cinderella who had been dancing with the Prince! She knew the slipper would fit Cinderella, so she locked Cinderella in her room.

Both stepsisters tried to cram their feet into the glass slipper, but it didn't fit them.

Just then, Cinderella broke out of her room. But before she could try on the slipper, it crashed to the floor. "Perhaps this will help," she said, pulling the other slipper out of her pocket.

Soon after, the Prince and Cinderella were married. Cinderella's dreams had finally come true because she never gave up trying to reach them.

Cinderella: A Story of Perseverance

Perseverance means never ever giving up! When something is important to you, you need perseverance to keep working to achieve your goal.

Cinderella's Stepmother and stepsisters did everything they could to cause her to give up. They were mean to her, gave her extra chores, destroyed her dress, and even tried locking her in her room. But Cinderella never quit! She knew she'd find happiness if she continued to work for it. With perseverance, Cinderella found all that she wanted and more.